Monster Trucks

Joy Keller

illustrations by Misa Saburi

GODWIN BOOKS

Henry Holt and Company ⛰ New York

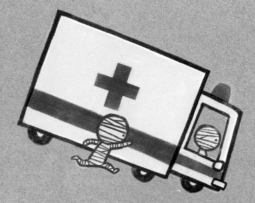

Henry Holt and Company
Publishers since 1866
175 Fifth Avenue, New York, New York 10010
mackids.com

Library of Congress Cataloging-in-Publication Data is available.
ISBN 978-1-62779-617-0

Our books may be purchased in bulk for promotional, educational,
or business use. Please contact your local bookseller or the Macmillan
Corporate and Premium Sales Department at (800) 221-7945 ext. 5442
or by e-mail at MacmillanSpecialMarkets@macmillan.com.

First edition—2017 / Designed by April Ward
The illustrations for this book were created with Adobe Photoshop.
Printed in China by RR Donnelley Asia Printing Solutions Ltd.,
Dongguan City, Guangdong Province

1 3 5 7 9 10 8 6 4 2

For Nikolas and Vivian, my little monsters

—J. K.

For my niece, Tamako

—M. S.

All monsters love the autumn air,
just right to sneak and spook and scare.
But other seasons of the year,
they shift into a different gear.

They put on boots and hats and vests
to do the work that they do best . . .
driving monster trucks!

The **werewolf** digs the deepest holes
for houses, pools, electric poles,
and also things that he enjoys—
like giant bones and squeaky toys.

You want a road that's smooth and new?
The **skeletons** are just the crew.
They pave and roll and put up cones
without a sweat—they're only bones.

The **yeti** likes to plow the snow,
especially when it's ten below.

To every blizzard, he's exposed—
he drives without the windows closed.

The **witch** trades in her trusty broom
for something with a bit more **vroom**.
She sweeps the streets and clears debris.
Her roadways sparkle brilliantly.

The grossest work for any truck
is hauling loads of slimy muck.
Swamp monster doesn't mind a bit.
She even stops to swim in it.

The **vampire** likes to hang up high
on cherry pickers in the sky.

He works on buildings at great heights
but never, **ever** changes lights.

Dozing dirt and rocks and trees
the Minotaur can do with ease.
Hard work won't make this bull forlorn.
(Just don't ask to honk his horn.)

The **ogre** angers easily
and goes on a destructive spree.

He loves to swing the **wrecking ball** and pummel buildings till they **fall**.

A speeding ambulance draws near.
A **mummy's** working in the rear.

He'll patch each monster
bump and scrape
with lots of bandages
and tape.

But when the full moon starts to rise,
the weary monsters rub their eyes.

It's time to park
the trucks in sheds
and head home to
their **monster beds**.

At rest in **YOUR** bed, tucked in tight,
don't fear these monsters in the night.

Beneath your staircase, bed, or chair—
you won't find **monsters** anywhere.

**They're much too tired
to crawl and creep.**

They're snoring soundly,
fast asleep.